My Very Tree

To all who appreciate and
enjoy reading

Crumps Barn Studio
Crumps Barn, Syde, Cheltenham GL53 9PN
www.crumpsbarnstudio.co.uk

Cover design and illustrations by Lorna Gray

Printed in Gloucestershire on FSC certified paper by Severn, a
carbon neutral company

ISBN 978-1-915067-07-4

My Very Tree

BEVERLEY GORDON

Collected Poems

Crumps Barn Studio

A BROTHER'S HATE: PART 1

Born into depths of sin as I work in anger
A hate rises within as I am born in sin
In the beating of the sun each day the hard work begins
Sacrifice I make to the God above
who has given us another chance in his love
But hate and anger grow within me
I could not see beyond the trees

What lies in the corner of my eyes, I behold what was
    once a paradise
I was told the story from my parents who are old
How they did not have to toil so hard and how life
    was sweet
The dew drops, the honeysuckle tree, the birds and
    the bees
The lion, the tiger, all these not forgetting the fruit trees
Yes life was sweet oh how I could cry
Two cherubs stationed by with the flaming sword
I cannot get in to peer into what was once a paradise
Nor would I want to try

I turn and look away, I see my young brother passing by
Not a care not a frown as he waves me by with a
      smug smile
His offering to God was his delight
I find no pleasure I find no joy
I will get rid of him once and for all
Angry, I am hate, I will destroy

A BROTHER'S HATE: PART 2

My brother, I call, let's go for a walk
Past the field of hay, in the bushes that's where I lay
    my brother
In death despair, in anger I am I have no care
When God asks where is my brother
Bitter I am, I say "am I my brother's keeper"
Weep I do not and continue on my way
But God says to me "what's this you have done
Your brother's blood cries out to me from the land"

Then I realise what I have done
I could no more turn back the sun
Much more bring my brother back
Sentenced I am to a land of despair
To be killed if anyone meets me there
I plead to God out of guilt and shame
This burden is hard to bear
He lovingly hears my plea
He sets a sign so I won't be harmed

My generation has grown but I come to no harm
But as I watch my generation grow
I see the destruction of my woe!
Throughout the land they have formed a weapon
of destruction

My generation will not stand to gain God's inheritance
Of the promised land. Oh! What have I done
Anger, hate, an inheritance sin that lies in wait
No way to run as I say farewell to the land that I stand on
Am I sorry?
Well you will never know as I lay in the ground below
For dust I am, dust I return
I am Cain. This is my story.

I WANT

Have you ever given thought about the words: I want
WANT is the hypnotising of the things in the world
Whether it may be objects or fleshly desire
Of what's in the world or what lays beyond
     our imagination
Whatever it is, it is so appealing to us so we WANT it
We do not look at the cost or the consequence we just
     know we WANT it
Our WANTS are activated by emotions that stir within us
So we act upon it to the point of no self-control.
The WANT of our eyes stirs that emotion we have
     no distraction
Like flies to a bright light not realising the danger
     that beholds us

OUR NEEDS

Our NEEDS is a must, a desired
The things we NEED to maintain a happy full life
A man sees the NEEDS of a wife
So he fulfils it. A wife sees the NEEDS of her husband so
She fulfils it.
This maintains a balance of life's desires
And so rejects the desire of the WANT
With this in mind you have saved time
With self-control you have saved your soul.

YOU WILL NEVER KNOW

You will never know how much I love you
You will never know how much I care
You will never know what lies beneath my teardrops
You will never know my dear

You will never know the pain I am in
You will never know if I lay awake at night or keep still
You will never know my dear you will never know

You will never know the amount of time I count the stars
Or watch the sun from afar
You will never know the distance I have travelled to get
    where you are
You will never know my dear you will never know

For there you lie you do not care
Your silence has given me the answer anyway
So you will never know my dear.
You will never know

AM I JUST A FOOL

Foolish I was to think you care
Foolish I was to think you'd be there
Foolish I was to try to share my thoughts
Foolish I was to give you the time of day
Foolish I was when I got the news
I reached out but you refused
A hand of friendship you did not choose
It's sad to ask but do you really care
Foolish I am to want the answer anyway.

WHO AM I

When no one is there for you I am
When you feel cold and have no one to keep you warm
I am
When your tears are falling and there is no one
to wipe them away
I am
When you are tired and weary and you have
no place to rest your head
I am
When you are sick and no one seem to care I am
I will always be there
Who am I?
I am love

DISTANCE LOVE

From a distance I have loved you
As the leaves fall from the tree and the snow is nowhere
To be seen I have loved you
In the dark of the day I have loved you
In the error of your ways I have loved you
In time of despair I have loved you
From the moon beyond the horizon I have loved you
Yet you are nowhere to be seen
A distance love that's all it is, there is no in between
Yet I have loved you.

IN MY MIND

We dance in the night right into the break of dawn
When the sun begins to rise
And the first chirping of the birds singing sweet melody
And the wind carries the fresh morning air

We dance back in time as we spin past 1999
We see no crime
Not even the devastation of the Cold War that took
      place in 1949
Hmm!! Not that I can really recall

Oops! What happened in 1854 I honestly do not know
So we continue dancing into 1704
Time was forever passing slow still I really did not know
We have gone so far back in time history just flows
But we kept on dancing through each door
What a way to go
Oh! Damn there is a knock on the door
The music stops the clock has come back
So there I was standing on the floor all alone.

WHO ARE YOU

I have no beginning I have no ending
I am here whenever I am needed
I make your heart beat
I just don't come round once a year or once a week
I am always here and everywhere
I bring joy not sorrow
I bring a bond of unity
I bring lasting happiness
I bring the best out of you not the worst
I am perfect in every way
I am the one that makes you glow
You all have me but you all do not know
Once you come to know me I will not go
Unless you choose the path that's always dark and cold
I really don't know
I am always here with a glow
My name is LOVE never ending flow

WHERE ARE YOU

Days have come nights have fallen
Yet I am still alone no arm to hold
No joy to be found only a teardrop beneath my frown
I long for the day when you will come
And no longer when a teardrop will be found

For your gentle smile your warm embrace will dry
        those tears
I long for the day when you can touch my face and say
Dear dear my child dry those tears

HIDE AWAY

You shut me out, you bolt the door
You close the window, you write on the door
No one lives here anymore
Your heart is broken so no more room to grow
A fabrication of lies, they draw a line
So you shut me out
You bolt the door
You close the window, you write on the door
A hidden file full of lies
No one lives here anymore, the heart is closed.

I RAISE YOU UP

I carried you in my womb for nine months
I have loved you before you were born
You kick around inside me
Your way of communicating I must agree
I rub my tummy to reassure you
It's ok it's ok
I feel you quietly fall asleep
So you see I know you well before you knew me

I hold you in my arms when you are born
I kiss your forehead to reassure you it's ok, I say it's ok
You then open your eyes for the first time and look at me
For that magical moment our eyes meet then you go
To sleep

A child of mine you are my beating heart
I watch you grow up from the very start
I am always by your side to catch you when you fall
And dry your tears, oh no not just that's all
There are times when you feel so sad
I would gladly try to fix that
But you'll be grounded if you do bad
A mother's love that's all

Stop!!!
It has become silent I then feel a rush of cold breeze
That brings me down on my knees
I pray to the Lord to give me the strength to keep
the peace
Is this a newborn disease?
One question please, can this be real?
I am now a victim of my own productive system
A child that was born to me is now my enemy
Can this be real, or am I really living a lie how
could this be
Is my mind playing tricks on me
My child has turned against me
My child looks at me as if I am the enemy
I raised my child with love
I taught my child to love not to destroy
But what goes through a child's mind and heart
I have no thoughts
I only know I have a broken heart.

A PROMISE IS A PROMISE

When you stood before God and friends, a promise
    you made to me
To love and honour and so the story went
But a hidden secret you did not tell
For your promise did not come to pass
You had your fingers crossed
For better it was at the start but your fingers
    were still crossed
But I trust in you still, worse was to come,
    I was not thrilled

You have now shown the colour of your will
Rich we were not, but we got by still
I kept my head up high you could not keep still
Poor began to crouch at the door
Please do not let it in I pleaded, I was ignored

A promise you did not keep for rich in every sense of
    life and love
Poor is what you give
Angry I was but chose to ignore

For better or for worse a promise I kept
My heart did not wander but my soul did not rest
You really put me to the test
Unkind and selfish you have become
You left out the love and honour and kept the rest
Which now brought on by stress
I can contest you have no respect
For the love I thought you have you lay to rest
No not on me but on someone else's chest

Now that you have been burnt at the waist
You have turned on me for the rest of the years
Your frustration of not getting your way
A promise you have made from the start
Not knowing your fingers were crossed
Please I ask of you, go your way
I cannot afford any more broken tears.

A CHILD IS BORN

A child born of a mother and father is an inheritance
      from God
A child becomes a companion
A reliant a confidant a friend
To their parent of age now old and grey

Who can they put their trust in if not their own
Who are able to feed them if their hands become
Too slow to reach their mouth
Or dry their tears or wipe their hands and face
Wash their feet when they cannot reach
Kiss them on their forehead or on their cheek
A reassurance, love, that's all a parent needs

But instead a nightmare of uncontrollable outrage
      they receive
A child has grown to care no more
They have forgotten what their parents have done for
      them before

They have now placed them in a home
A strange place that they do not know
A place of many strangers if the truth be told
A place with iron bars and locked doors
That's how it feels for those who do not know
A child does not care anymore
They forgot the love they once had before
With parents that have grown old
Oh! What a way to go.

NO FRIENDSHIP AT ALL

I won't knock I won't call
I won't laugh I won't talk
I know now you do not want to know
Crazy it may sound
I realised just a moment ago
My messages you have ignored
So I will not knock I will not call
I will stay far
A distance memory is all I will recall.

I REMEMBER

I woke up each and every morning with your stale breath
Blowing across my face I would smile and say no disgrace
Then I would kiss your forehead and make you a
      cup of tea

I remember the footprints we made in the snow
Like two schoolchildren
I would fall, you were there to catch me

I remember the time I missed my train
It was dark but you were right there
To accept my call
You dried my tears with the warmth of your voice
And kept me company on the line

I remember when I packed your lunch
Each day I would write a note simply saying
      MY RAINBOW
You would text and say that will do dear that will do

I remember you were late getting home
Your car had broken down
It was wet and cold then the rain began to fall
You were not answering your phone at all
I could not reach you, you were all alone
I wanted to come and find you but where would I start
So I stood by the window in the dark
Then there you were no car sad and cold
I raced into your arms and wrapped you in a blanket to
      keep you warm
No need for words but action said it all
I kept you in my arms where you fell asleep
As night falls and dawn breaks I remember it all
You are so near yet so far

I REMEMBER:
PART 2

Do you remember the holiday we took
It was meant to be a weekend away
But you could not stay work had called you away
But I did so much want you to stay

Do you remember walking along the shore-way
You would kick the sand up in the air
We did not care as we watched the wave
Do you remember we flew the kite
Against the night wind we must have been mad
But we kept going still

Do you remember climbing on the rock
I was shocked as a wasp stung you on your back
Do you remember when we had a picnic in the dark
Oh we were so daft so we started to laugh
For we forgot the knife and fork
So chopsticks we made from bark near the lake
Do you remember
I remember them all so well.

NOWHERE TO HIDE

Away you go run when God's judgement a come
Away you go run when you hear the trumpet sound
Away you go run when tomorrow don't come
Tick tock tick tock the clock runs

The time has come mankind can't run
They call rock to tumble down cover them to the ground
Darkness falls no star in the sky
Man tries to turn on the light
Power cut far and wide no light

Away you go run when God's judgement a come
Away you go run when the trumpet a sound
Away you go run run run run
Gunshot weapon of massive destruction
Can't wipe out God's nuclear reaction
A way you go run when God's judgement a come,
        come, come

REFLECTIONS

I look in the mirror what do I see
Oh! It's only me a reflection of my past
Present and future staring back at me
Past is the sadness in my eyes
Present is myself looking at me
Future is my smile of happiness
Of what lies before me.

SHADOW

I am just a shadow that gets ignored
You find me crawling on the floor
Blink and I'll be on the door
I am just a shadow that everyone ignores
You would step on me but you would not know
I am just a shadow that gets ignored.

CAN YOU SEE

I know you, you know me not
I hear you, you hear me not
I see you, you see me not
The blind are not blind
That they cannot hear
The deaf are not deaf that they
Cannot see
Invisible I am to you the naked eyes
In silence I stay all by myself
in the smell of the warm night air
I know you, you know me not
Through the dark clouds and the rainfall
I see you, you see me not
As the tree carries the whisper of the wind
From all distant parts of the land
I hear you, you hear me not.

REVELATION

Revelation is a celebration of the newborn nation
Acclimatization of justification
Now all the nation will have to know
Revelation, proclamation
God's destination the seven bowls of salvation
Against the wicked of this generation
All tribes and tongue have no place to run
When the Angels there a beat their drum
Almighty God's son a come with the sword
Of salvation

So I say revelation tribulation celebration
Justification a message to all the nation
JAH!!!

MY CONSCIENCE AND ME

Conscience: would you not agree that you are your
        worst enemy
Me: no. I would not agree that I am my worst enemy
Now why would you go and say a thing like that to me?
Conscience: would you not agree when life gives you
        a lemon
The saying is you should make lemonade.
Me: no I would not agree, when life gives me a lemon
I should make lemonade, I will wash my meat instead
Conscience: wow! You stupid me
Me: Well excuse me, you are quite rude indeed.
Conscience: would you not agree you take life too
        seriously
Me: no I would not agree that I take life too seriously
Knock knock, knock knock!
Conscience: what!!
Me: why could the chicken not cross the bridge?
Conscience: I do not know why the chicken could not
        cross the bridge
Me: because he was already on the other side
Conscience: stupid indeed
(Hey come here, between you and me
That was funny but cannot let Me know)

Me: see I do not take life too seriously

Conscience: would you not agree you are stupid indeed

Me: no I would not agree that I am stupid indeed
please refrain from

Using that word

Conscience: what word

Me: that word the one you want me to repeat

I am not stupid indeed I will not repeat.

Conscience: you so right, clever little me.

Me: are you mocking me, you are my Conscience

To direct me to keep me safe from harm

But instead you are mocking me.

Conscience: oh lighten up can you not see

You take life too seriously

I will train you to be a better part of me.

Me: who me? In your dreams I think you are my
worst enemy.

Conscience: I am done.

Me: I will find a new Conscience for you are too
mean to me

Conscience: now I am really done. No words

ANOTHER DAY FOR A GOOD RACE

Good morning high good morning low
Hello Mr Willow how does the wind blow
It's a fine day for a race today I wonder
How well will it go?

Gather round time to put on a show
A water race you all do know
The snake the fox and the hippos too
A relay race is now about to take place

Mr Snake are you ready to race
Where is Mrs Crow you all ought to know
Mr Snake open your mouth spit her out
the game is not hide and seek

Fly high Mrs Crow and keep a close eye down below
Miss Owl hoot when ready
Mr Horse stand still keep steady
Mr Swan what is wrong
You've got to stand on the bank
Where is Mrs Goose. Her kids are on the loose
Oh what a day, catch those mini geese today

Mr Goose take her place
Now what do you say
What do you mean you cannot swim
But, but, oh what a day
Mr Lizard take her place.
What do you mean the water is cold today.
Well jump on a leaf and paddle away
All the birds are on the tree waiting impatiently

Miss Owl hoot away let's get this race on the way
Ready set go

Mr Snake don't hold on to Mr Fox's tail
You are holding him back let him go
All the animals are laughing
Even the pigeon falls on the ground
Mr Hippo what are you doing you are not moving
What do you mean your hoof is stuck
The hyenas are rolling on the ground their laughter
        out of control

Mr Swan why are you still on the bank
Mr Lizard is still going slow, paddle Mr Lizard
        paddle away
Mr Swan is still on the bank
Mr Lizard you are going the wrong way
No! Come back, you're going the wrong way
Mr Horse let him grab your tail, swing him back this way
I just cannot look, where is he? Mr Lizard cannot be seen
Ooh he has caught on the tree
Oh Mr Lizard come here to me lie on my lap go to sleep
The sun is going down what can I say this race was not
        meant to be
Let's call it a day.

Hey hey Miss Narrator
What happened to Mr Fox and snake
The hippo the horse, is Mr Swan still on the bank?
Who won the race?
Narrator: are you still here did you not hear
We called it a day.

LISTEN

Silent is a doorway that leads you to nowhere
It gives no light it just keeps you in a straight line

Silent is a doorway that leads you to nowhere
There is no compromise, it does not reason
It does not recognise that you are left in the dark

Silent is a doorway that leads to nowhere
It cannot comprehend, it does not let you understand
It's a right pain in your head
It takes you down a narrow road that leaves you so
        damp and cold
Then you realise, it has left you all alone

Silent is a doorway that lead you to nowhere
Wow! wow!! Stop
What are you saying silent is a doorway that leads
        to nowhere
What does that even mean?
It means I don't want to speak to you
Can you not take a hint.

MR BEE SPEAK IN POETRY

In my very tree
Hello Mr Bee, what are you doing? Poetry, well I never!
Please tell it to me (so he caught some and is ready
      to speak)
You see I have been observing some of these insects
All around me.
The wasp so gallant and fine, but has a sting
That will hurt your behind.

The centipede crawls along the floor looking for bugs
To crunch but could find no more
The spider with his long legs spins the longest web
Only to trip over it and land himself on the floor

How am I doing so far
Oh wonderful please continue
(As he caught some more)
The fly goes on a date oh how he loved that bright light
He never came back that night
The stick insect he stayed too long in the sun
He did not listen to anyone, he was well done
Oh! My goodness Mr Bee what terrible tragedy

What about you Mr Bee
Who me, well now as shy as I can be
I give good honey off my tree but you have to ask me
First with a please, for you well know I sting like a bee.
But you are a bee
That's right
Well Mr Bee that was lovely to be in your company knee,
        you get it?
Company knee hahaha
Mr Bee shakes his head and flies away instead
That bee had no sense of humour
Did you all get my joke?
No!!

ARE YOU LISTENING

Are you listening to me, go to the shop across at the light
    if you please
Take this change and buy me a quarter of cheese
On the way pass the bakery, a loaf of bread a dozen eggs
Then walk along the road, ahead a farmer's market you
    will see
Get me a stick of celery if you please
Are you listening to me
Then turn around and come back quick
I will get a fire to light my stick
I have a very hungry belly, would you like me to repeat
Are you listening to me
Mr Monkey do you realise you are talking to a tree
Where are your glasses please
Mr Monkey looks at me as if I am crazy
You won't find no shop around this land
Not even a busy road for you to step out on
Not like the city where you came from
Why don't you have a banana bread instead

It may seem silly to you in your very tree
But I overheard bee speaking in poetry

So I thought if bee can speak poetry then so can all of we
So I don't want a banana bread
So kindly keep your thoughts to yourself
Wow he is in a mood how rude indeed
I will just go back in and close my door.

A MOTHER'S LOVE IS CRUEL

You treated her so cruel, you like to beat her behind
You did not hold back from using the strap
If it was not that it would be a pan a shoe
Or what you can find, your anger blazes on her back
You show no mercy for her back
You pull her hair when she tries to run from your lash
She cries out stop stop!
It's not her fault she reminded you of your
Great rich aunt with long hair down her back
Rich and posh
Your hate for her was beyond control so the story has
        been told
Now you have a child which everyone call throwback
Because she now looks like that great rich aunt
That child, that was born from you
Rich she was not, was she poor yes
You made sure of that
You fed her cheese when others have a meal
The only inheritance she has from you
Is her hair so long down her back
Even though hate and anger still linger on
You do not stop
She tries to fight back, so she gives you a slap
She finally is able to take her stand
From a mother's cruel hand

WHAT DO YOU MEAN TO ME

From the womb of my mother you have kept me safe
You travel through life watching over me
No you did not hide your face
You stood the test of time in its rightful place
You have watched me grow from there to now
Through the storm of my life you have stretched out
     your hands
Yet my grip was not strong
So fall I did "ouch"!! I have only myself to blame
But you came again hand of mercy you extended
My grip was not tight enough
Fall I did once more
I have given up
Again you came extended your hand of mercy
Yet stubborn and hurt I chose to ignore
Reject your hand I did
You left me alone so I think
Again I kept falling my anger grew
Bitter I became but that did not matter
Because I kept falling and falling
But still you were there patiently waiting
I called to you but you did not answer
I cried to you but you did not dry my tears
But you are always there
Yet you seem so far away
So I think
Now I stop to think have I done you wrong

[Pause]

The penny drops
You were there all along it was for my heart to
     grow strong
Then you stretch out your hand to show me your life plan
I begin to learn all I can about you and your life plan
Listen and learn I accept your hand
With strong grip as tight as I can
Now I am here to give others a helping hand
Through your undeserved kindness now I
     fully understand
Thank you my God Jehovah for you truly understand.

MOTHER KNOWS BEST

Mother please do not put me to the test
You act as if you know best
I fall you laugh and say get up dry your tears, a little fall
    won't hurt you at all
When I was your age I fell all the time, cracked head,
    scraped knees, fractured wrist
Come on you kids are soft today
Go on go out and play
But mother dearest it's going to rain I will get wet and
    catch a cold
My shoes will be wet. Oh! I do not know
Say what! Now you my child what are you talking about
A little rain is nothing on your head
When I was your age I had no shoe to fit my foot
So I would run and jump and chase the rain, wet I was
    from head to toe
It was fun time I did not worry about a cold
Toughen up my child and go and play in the rain
Take your shampoo
Why mother why
It's free water wash your hair
Oh boy!! Mother knows best.

EYES LIKE BLUE DIAMONDS

Eyes like blue diamonds, a smile that captivates the heart
And so the spirit flows on a journey, a journey into space
Where there is no time, no ticking clock, no rush of noise
Silence as I watch the stars, still seen from afar

Eyes like blue diamonds, a smile that captivates the heart
Floating on the clouds I have no wings
I am not a bird but I watch from a distance
Listen can you hear it, the whisper of the wind
Circling around me.
Who are you? Who are you? It keeps whispering
I keep silent as I close my eyes, I dare not open them
The force of the wind pushes me here it pushes me
  over there
Still no sound I make, as a teardrop falls from my eye
"Hush now" A ray of sunshine says to the cold wind
I raise my head up, not daring to open my eyes
You are far from home the warm breezy ray of
  sunshine whispers

Eyes like blue diamond, a smile that captivates the heart
I whisper
Eyes like blue diamond, a smile that captivates the heart
I keep repeating
This is unreachable you must return home now instead it
        whispers
Darkness falls as I look beyond the horizon. What
        happens next I cannot tell.

A STORM IS COMING

The wind has picked up, there is a cloud overhead
Has anyone seen little Robin Red Breast?
Come come now, no time to slack.
A storm is coming look ahead
Gather the young ones out of their nest
Mr Mole you have to quickly burrow more hole
So you all can be underground
Come along now before it's too late
That reminds me was I not baking a cake
Mr Snake dive down below let the fishes know
Not to come up they must swim
Into the cave there they will be safe
Mr Crow sound the alarm squawk loud as you never did
      before
Mr Monkey don't get grumpy, get the chimps out of the
      tree
Lead them into the cave next to me
Mr Mole it's starting to get cold let the toad into the hole
Then help all the little insects in
Mrs Swan come along gather your little ones
Mr and Mrs Hippo follow the fishes down below
There will be room enough hurry now don't be slow
Has anyone yet seen little Robin. Oh! Where did that
      little bird go?
Ah there you are snake is everyone in the water cave safe
Please get up the tree and bring the birds nests to me

My treehouse will stand but it's best to have my feet on
        the land
Head count if you please Mr Fox
The storm is now over the land
The wind has picked up speed now the rain has begun
But the sky is dark no more. Fox hold the phone.
But I don't have one, it's just a saying please understand
What have you noticed about this storm that's begun
Have I told you the story of old (pause as they all shake
        their head, No they said)
Oh no everyone gather round we have spent so much
        time having fun
We have forgotten the storm was to come, it brings the
        rain to sweep the land.
Sit right here gather round light the fire oh Mr Monkey
        are you still being grumpy
This is how the story goes – the storm comes along to
        clean up the land
To bring back nature to its best,
So all things on the land can be refreshed
So you will once again see nature at its best
Then the rain beats the land like a drum
Down below the water will flow, a current runs through
        the water
Did you not know
Cleaning everything that was once new now is old

The trees and the plants are in distress
But the sun comes along and oh how they are blessed
By the warmth that even the little buds come to life
And the sunflowers open wide
The daffodils and the tulips have great big smiles
Not forgetting the dandelions who can be so shy
And so the doctor bird goes to work, examining
Each and every plant
Whilst the bees do their best dance getting a real
        buzzing speed
Then off they go oh my plenty of honey will flow
yum yum.
That's the story that was once told

ESCAPE INTO YOUR IMAGINATION

I know you all may believe it or not,
I come from a land divided and cold
where love is bought with silver and gold
And nature has no place to call home
So I found this place so I can escape
Yet I am not really far from what I would call home

It's a place where nature runs free and all the animals
    can live in peace
I have my own very tree it overlooks the land far and
    beyond
I would describe it to you but that is my secret recipe

Some birds do live with me, well, in my tree
We have fun in the sun but we don't stay too long
We still have plenty of work to be done
You see when I am sad and low and have nowhere to go
This land that I have come to understand is created by
    my own
Imaginative mind, it's no crime, to want to escape
To a place where love flows and nature is free to grow
And the animals run free and don't step on each
    other's toes
OK not toes well how about nose.

You are never too young or old to find a place
That you can call your own
In your very mind that only you can go where
Happiness and love come to life
If you want to go to space to explore, your mind is your
     front door
If you want to fly a plane your adventure is your own
Perhaps take a friend or two along for the ride.
It's your story that has never been told
Well I hope you have
Enjoyed the time you have spent with me in my mind

Miss Narrator
Wait ,wait what happened to little Robin
And did you ever get to bake that cake,
(Miss Narrator smiles)
That's another adventure for when you come back.

MY VERY TREE

I am not Alice in wonderland
I do not go down a rabbit hole where fantasy and
    chaos go on
I am me in my very tree where each day the birds
    gather to hear my story of long ago
By afternoon the deer, the mole, the rabbit, the lion,
    even the bear sit with me
As we watch from under the tree
the birds race each one against the wind
Some fly high some fly low
Little Robin Red Breast hitches a ride on the wing of
    the Eagle
Clever little robin
All the animals come to see
Oops open your eyes Mr Bear it's ok dear little Robin
    did not fall
The falcon and the crow stop to strike a pose as the
    sparrow flies above their nose
The falcon grabs the sparrow's wing and swings him
    back to the beginning
The sparrow was not impressed he races towards the
    falcon's chest
The crow ducks down the sparrow misses his head
Stop!!
I shout from the ground get it together now I am
    not impressed

Pigeon stop being a chicken the race is yours to take
      first place
You've just got to be brave get out of your nest
Of course the wind is strong be brave and glide along
Mr Wind be gentle please give these birds time to
      spread their wings
Now let the race begin
All the animals on the ground lift their heads and
      cheer aloud
As the sun goes down to bed it's time for all
Sleepy-heads to say a happy good night
Come along Mr Bear tomorrow is another racing day

Wait wait wait
Hello Miss Narrator
Who won the race?
We will find out who took first place as the sun comes
      up tomorrow dear

PRAYER

Prayer is a wonderful thing we have in the universe today
It brings us together in a unique way
When disaster comes our way, everyone gathers to pray

Forget about Batman and Robin, Superman even
      Spider-man
Those are characters of someone else's imaginary mind

Prayer is the hero of the day
When you are sick you pray
When you are hungry you pray
When you need comfort you pray
When you go for a job you pray

Before you eat you pray
You pray before you go to bed
You pray when you wake up and be thankful
For another day
Are you getting the idea?
Prayer is a wonderful thing we have today
Many may disagree
But watch them fall in a hole, see if they don't pray
For someone to rescue them that very day

When death comes to a person do many not call the
        priest to pray
Prayer is a wonderful thing we have today
So log it on your calendar or in your phone
Just remember there is no set time to pray
It is our hero in a unique way
So do not forget to pray
It saves lives each and every day

WHY DO I WRITE

I write for joy, some write for fun
It's a way to escape this misery
As well as to use one's imagination, can you understand
In this world that we belong to it's cold and damp not
     much going on
Joy and happiness can hardly be found
So I find a world to escape within
Where chaos and violence don't belong
It's a world that you can build to see how life could be
Where birds are not caged and there are no mental
     disabilities
People are free to work in harmony
With the birds and bees and all the wild animals
Can't you see
And at times we bring it alive, for everyone to enjoy
So you see writing is a comfort to me
I feel safe in my own realities
I have a mind that is full of hope and joy
So leave me be and let me write and enjoy.

A Note from the Author

Life was never sweet – growing up bad memories were
all I had

My first encounter with a teacher as a little nipper wasn't
nice. He used to get us to lower our heads on our desks
and close our eyes, while he went round to each person's
desk and stole something from their lunch bag that their
mother had made. I used to watch him from the corner
of my eye.

Then I grew a bit older and moved to another school,
only now I was with bigger kids

Well, they seemed bigger at the time, but it turns out
that I was very tiny – in height and size

Times were hard, my parents moved to England and we
were raised by our grandma

Yes I was with my siblings

We had an aunty and uncle who treated us well. But one
was so unkind, she is very old now and now looks to me
for help. How easy she forgets.

But I have to forgive. It does not benefit me to hold on
to an unkind past.

I would go to school with not a whole book or pencil

It would be cut in half. That was all the good aunty could afford. Uncle made sure that on Special Holidays I did not get left out. My shoes lasted for a very long time for I would take them off after School and run home so I would have pretty shoes for church.

There was no TV but a radio that we would gather around to listen to.

The work on the land was very hard – there was hardly any time to have some fun

I was the only one that could climb the trees to pick the fruit that no one could reach not even with a stick

Gather firewood, carry water on my head. We all had a share in that

But as for school I would get 10 slaps with the biggest thickest belt you ever did see

We all were asked to spell flour – not seen that word before nor was I given it to learn

I spelled flowers, I was given 10 hard slaps 5 in each hand

I even now could hear the teacher across the other size of the room begging mercy on my behalf.

My teacher did not stop.

As the teardrops rolled down my cheek, I took
that beating

Each day I went to school, I would climb a tree,
never went to class

I would let my imagination run astray waiting for the
school bell to go off

As I grew, my imagination grew too – it kept me out
of most trouble

I would imagine what life would be like flying on a
cloud. I would talk to the caterpillars, even the trees
and the breeze, and dance in the rain.

At night as I went to bed, I would tell stories to my
siblings, those sleepy heads

Then I found the one thing that could calm my soul

God for he is truly real.

Now I use my imagination for others to enjoy my
stories in poetry

Yep! That's me.

About the Author

Beverley Gordon is the author of four poetry collections: *My Very Tree, Letters From Your Neighbour Far Away* and its sequel *From Your Neighbour In A Distant Land,* and *Love Covers All Things.*

She is a mother and grandmother, and lives and works in London.